P9-DXS-969

Aphids are very small insects.
They suck the juice from leaves,
and then the leaves die.
Ladybugs eat aphids.
That's good for trees, shrubs, and
other plants that have leaves.
To the ladybugs I have dedicated this book.
Three cheers for them!

No part of this publication may be reproduced in whole or in part, or stored in a retrieval system, or transmitted in any form or by any means, electronic, mechanical, photocopying, recording, or otherwise, without written permission of the publisher. For information regarding permission, write to HarperCollins Publisher, 10 East 53rd Street, New York, NY 10022.

ISBN 0-590-13066-8

Copyright secured 1977 in countries signatory to International Copyright Union.
All rights reserved. Published by Scholastic Inc., 555 Broadway, New York, NY 10012, by arrangement with HarperCollins Publishers.

SCHOLASTIC and associated logos are trademarks and/or registered trademarks of Scholastic Inc.

12 11 10 9 8 7 6 5 4 3   7 8 9/9 0 1 2/0

Printed in the U.S.A.   08

First Scholastic printing, September 1997

3K135000013485

The Grouchy Ladybug

Eric Carle

ST JUDE OF THE LAKE SCHOOL
600 MAHTOMEDI AVE
MAHTOMEDI, MN 55115

Scholastic Inc.

New York   Toronto   London   Auckland   Sydney

It was night and some fireflies danced around the moon.

At five o'clock in the morning the sun came up.
A friendly ladybug flew in from the left. It saw a leaf with many aphids on it,
and decided to have them for breakfast.
But just then a grouchy ladybug flew in from the right.
It too saw the aphids and wanted them for breakfast.

ST JUDE OF THE LAKE SCHOOL
600 MAHTOMEDI AVE
MAHTOMEDI, MN 55115

"Good morning," said the friendly ladybug.
"Go away!" shouted the grouchy ladybug. "I want those aphids."
"We can share them," suggested the friendly ladybug.
"No. They're mine, all mine," screamed the grouchy ladybug.
"Or do you want to fight me for them?"

"If you insist," answered the friendly ladybug sweetly.
It looked the other bug straight in the eye.
The grouchy ladybug stepped back.
It looked less sure of itself.
"Oh, you're not big enough for me to fight," it said.
"Then why don't you pick on somebody bigger?"
"I'll do that!" screeched the grouchy ladybug.
"I'll show you!" It puffed itself up and flew off.

At six o'clock
it met a yellow jacket.
"Hey you," said
the grouchy ladybug.
"Want to fight?"
"If you insist," said
the yellow jacket,
showing its stinger.
"Oh, you're not
big enough," said
the grouchy ladybug
and flew off.

At seven o'clock
it met a stag beetle
"Hey you," said
the grouchy ladybu
"Want to fight?"
"If you insist," said
the stag beetle,
opening its jaws.
"Oh, you're not
big enough," said
the grouchy ladybu
and flew off.

At eight o'clock
it came across
a praying mantis.
"Hey you," said
the grouchy ladybug.
"Want to fight?"
"If you insist," said
the praying mantis,
reaching out with
its long front legs.
"Oh, you're not
big enough," said
the grouchy ladybug
and flew off.

At nine o'clock
it almost flew into
a sparrow.
"Hey you," said
the grouchy ladybug.
"Want to fight?"
"If you insist," said
the sparrow, opening
its sharp beak.
"Oh, you're not
big enough," said
the grouchy ladybug
and flew off.

At ten o'clock
it saw a lobster.
"Hey you," said
the grouchy ladybug.
"Want to fight?"
"If you insist," said
the lobster,
stretching its claws.
"Oh, you're not big enough,"
said the grouchy ladybug
and flew off.

At eleven o'clock
it bumped into a skunk.
"Hey you," said
the grouchy ladybug.
"Want to fight?"
"If you insist," said
the skunk, starting to lift its tail.
"Oh, you're not big enough,"
said the grouchy ladybug
and flew off.

At twelve noon
it spotted a boa constrictor.
"Hey you," said
the grouchy ladybug.
"Want to fight?"
"If you insis-s-s-t," said the snake,
"right after lunch."
"Oh, you're not big enough,"
said the grouchy ladybug
and flew off.

At one o'clock
it happened upon
a hyena.
"Hey you," said
the grouchy ladybug.
"Want to fight?"
"If you insist," said the hyena,
laughing eerily and
showing its teeth.
"Oh, you're not big enough,"
said the grouchy ladybug
and flew off.

At two o'clock
it met a gorilla.
"Hey you," said
the grouchy ladybug.
"Want to fight?"
"If you insist," said the gorilla,
beating its chest.
"Oh, you're not big enough,"
said the grouchy ladybug
and flew off.

At three o'clock
it ran into
a rhinoceros.
"Hey you," said
the grouchy ladybug.
"Want to fight?"
"If you insist," said
the rhinoceros,
lowering its horn.
"Oh, you're not big enough,"
said the grouchy ladybug
and flew off.

At four o'clock
it encountered
an elephant.
"Hey you," said
the grouchy ladybug.
"Want to fight?"
"If you insist," said the elephant,
raising its trunk and
showing its big tusks.
"Oh, you're not big enough,"
said the grouchy ladybug
and flew off.

At five o'clock
it met a whale.
"Hey you," said
the grouchy ladybug.
"Want to fight?"
But the whale
did not answer at all.
"You're not
big enough anyway,"
said the grouchy ladybug
and flew off.

At five fifteen the grouchy ladybug said to one of the whale's flippers, "Hey you, want to fight?"

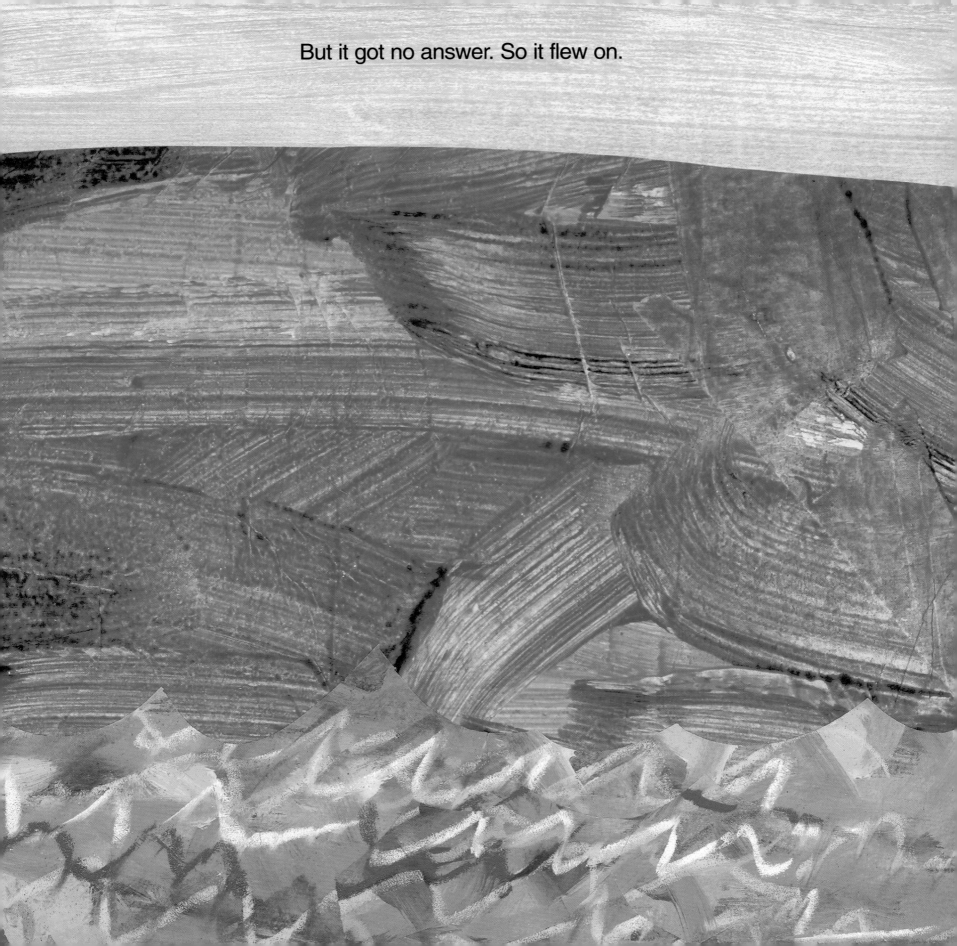

But it got no answer. So it flew on.

At five thirty the grouchy ladybug said to the whale's fin, "Hey you, want to fight?"

But it got no answer. So it flew on.

At a quarter to six the grouchy ladybug said to the whale's tail, "Hey you, want to fight?"

And the whale's tail gave
the grouchy ladybug
such a SLAP . . .

. . . that it flew across the sea and across the land.

At six o'clock the grouchy ladybug arrived right back where it had started from.

"Ah, here you are again," said the friendly ladybug. "You must be hungry. There are still some aphids left. You can have them for dinner."
"Oh, thank you," said the wet, tired, and hungry ladybug.

Soon all the aphids were gone.
"Thank you," said the leaf.
"You are welcome," answered both ladybugs, and they went to sleep.
The fireflies, who had been sleeping all day, came out to dance around the moon.